THE
BORNINGROOM

THE
BORNINGROOM

PAUL FLEISCHMAN

SCHOLASTIC INC.
New York Toronto London Auckland Sydney

ISBN 0-590-46043-9

12 11 10 9 8 7 6 5 4 3 2 1   3 4 5 6 7 8/9

Printed in the U.S.A.   28

First Scholastic printing, January 1993

*To Steve and Elizabeth Willborn,
and to Emily, Anne, and Jane*

THE
BORNINGROOM

I

Four small walls, sheathed with pine, painted white. A window. A door onto the kitchen, for warmth. Two chairs. A bed, nearly filling up the room, like a bird held in cupped hands. Standing by the bed, squire beside his knight, a table bearing a Bible and a lamp. I'm certain you've stood in many such rooms.

Look out the window. That's a sugar maple. Grandfather greatly cherished that tree. Now tilt your head back and look up at the beams. You can still make out the track of his plane. He'd put it, and everything else that would fit, and his wife and baby into a wagon and set out from New Hampshire in the year 1820. He'd heard there was plenty of land in Ohio and that corn and wheat would leap out of the soil if a man merely tickled it with his hoe. When he got here, he was glad he'd brought his ax as well. Ohio was a forest. He steered his oxen along the Stillwater, halted them here, and commenced cutting trees as if he were the avenging arm of the Lord. But when he came to that maple, it so put him in mind of New Hampshire, of his mother and father and sisters, all left behind, that he let it stand and decided to build his house beside it, for summer shade. He called it his memory tree.

He hauled his straightest oaks seven miles to a mill on Pig Creek and came home with planks. Being a New Englander, he raised up a New England house, with a stone-lined cellar and a long north roof, a smoke room for meats, a loom room for weaving. And behind the kitchen, as in his New Hampshire home, a borning room, set aside for both dying and giving birth—the room my father was born in before the window glass had yet arrived.

It's not a room that's seen much use. But the times it has stand up in my memory more than the months and years in between. Most of my life's turnings have taken place here.

It was on a snowy morning in January that Mama whispered to Father to ride for Mrs. Radtke, the midwife. Mama's last baby had been stillborn and the one before had died at two months. Following her mother's advice, which arrived in weekly letters from Baltimore, she'd all but concealed her condition this time. She'd scarcely spoken about the coming baby. She'd sewn not one piece of clothing for it. The afternoon before, when Father had brought the cradle down from the garret, she'd silently motioned him to return it. Outside, snow streamed out of the sky. Ignoring her pains, Mama cooked breakfast for the family, then began mixing dough. It was Saturday, her baking day. While the bread loaves rose, she churned butter with one hand and sorted seeds for spring planting with the other, giving the fates no sign that she was engaged in anything other than her chores. It was hours before Mrs. Radtke arrived. She found Mama lying in the borning room, the churn drawn up beside the bed and her right hand weakly working the handle.

Her waters finally broke about noon. That very instant she heard an owl call and then another answer back. She told the midwife how strange it was to hear owls hooting at midday. Mrs. Radtke replied that they were in truth the spirits of Mama's last two babies. Her pains came on in earnest then. Mama didn't dare moan or cry out, but just gripped the handle of the churn. Then a bird, small and black, struck the window with a bang. Mama jerked. There was a flash of huge wings. Maybe it was that shock that caused her the following moment to release her baby into Mrs. Radtke's hands.

"Ein Mädchen," she told Mama. "A fine girl." Above the baby's crying, she explained that a bird who gets into the house brings a death, that as soon as she'd come she'd had Father check for any open or broken windows, and that the bird hadn't even cracked the glass.

"Where is it?" asked Mama.

"Die Eulen," she answered. "The owls. One of them snatched it right up. They're watching over you both, it's sure. *Ja, ja.* This child, she'll live."

It was said that I had Mama's mother's high forehead and delicate fingers. Mama picked out all of our names. As if to enroll me at once among the living, within a quarter hour of my birth Father opened the family Bible, dipped a pen in ink, and wrote out "Georgina Caroline Lott, born the 11th day of January, 1851."

Two dozen times, two thousand times, Mama told this story—for the reason that I asked for it that often. "Yes, my dove, I recollect the day quite well," she'd always begin. "Snowflakes filled the sky thick as locusts." And slowly she'd repeat it once more, while our paring knives peeled or the spinning wheel whirred. She never lost patience with my requests, I suppose because she never lost gratitude that Mrs. Radtke had been right. I had lived.

2

I was with my friend Hattie Puckett, far out in her cornfield. "Listen!" she hissed. There was a rumble. "Thunder!" She peered at me. "And you know what that means."

I shook my head.

She lowered her voice. "It means somebody's fixing to die."

A grasshopper lit upon my shoulder, as if marking me as the victim.

"Lightning's the Lord sawing planks for the coffin," said Hattie. "Thunder's him hammering it together. When the rain comes down, he's commenced to paint it. Then he hunts out someone hiding sin in their heart—and slays 'em right where they stand."

I clutched my braids. I'd never heard this before. Hattie was a great dispenser of knowledge. Then another rumble, farther off, sounded. Hattie considered. "It's headed east," she said. "Most likely someone out toward Lanesville."

This came as a great relief to me. I knew not a soul in Lanesville. Neither did Hattie. Gaily, we pressed ahead, running, stumbling, skipping, singing, until we reached the watermelon patch Hattie had planted among the cornstalks. She sliced up a small melon with the knife she'd brought, and we both sat down and ate. It was July. I was sweat-soaked and limp as laundry. Hattie spit out a mouthful of seeds.

"I don't guess you know where babies come from," she said.

I was eight and a half, read well, and could cipher. But Hattie was nine, as she mentioned often, and regarded herself as a missionary sent to lift me from ignorance. She exhibited a melon seed on her palm.

"They come," she declared, "from these."

My eyebrows jerked. I examined the seed for signs of human resemblance while she described how a baby would grow in my stomach if I swallowed one after I'd married. Mama clearly hadn't taken care. Her belly was as big as a rain barrel. The baby, she'd said, would be born that summer.

Hattie tucked the seed in a pocket, swore me to secrecy, and leaned close. "I'm going to put it in the middle of a blackstrap muffin," she whispered. "Then I'll make sure my ma eats it. I want to have a little baby to hold, just like your mama's giving you."

I didn't reveal my own secret, that I half hoped Mama's baby would never be born. It felt strange to be withholding this from Hattie. And when she asked why I wasn't in school that summer, I told her that Mama thought I should wait, amazed to now hear myself lying outright. Mama, I knew, had encouraged me to go. But I'd seen her sewing for the coming baby and had watched her gently stroke her stomach. Her mother had written her that the older a woman was, the safer the delivery. The fear that had surrounded my birth had lifted. Mama publicly deliberated over names. Lately she'd seemed hardly to see me. If I began to leave her for school just as the new baby was born, would she not forget me entirely?

We headed back between the rows of corn. "I hope no raccoons ever find that patch," said Hattie. "Or runaway slaves."

11

I knew there was slavery just across the Ohio and had heard of the Underground Railroad, but I'd never set eyes on a runaway.

"My daddy says they slink through by the score," she said. "Last night he rode out with some men. They stopped two wagons. Didn't find any slaves hiding in 'em, though." I stared at her, shocked, and wondered if she knew that Father and Grandfather were devoted readers of the *Liberator*, the abolitionist newspaper.

"If they do," she said, "the law's on their side. Just knowing where one is and not turning him in is a crime. Six months in prison. My daddy knows the law up and down."

We emerged from the cornfield and parted ways, her wave more energetic than mine. Hattie was my dearest friend. I had four brothers and sisters but they were all older, and Hattie's was the only house within a mile of mine. We'd played since before my memory began, but this time our visit had left me troubled.

I soon spied our house, shaded by our maple, the two drawn close like a mare and colt. Mama was out on the porch. When I got there she slowly turned me around in a circle, drawing bits of tassel from my hair. "There now," she said. "It *is* our Georgina."

She was tall and lively-eyed, her hair dark as vanilla. Her fingers were gentle. I liked the feel of them roaming my hair, and wished she weren't through. She kissed the top of my head and strode toward the kitchen. I followed and helped her pit cherries.

At supper, I asked Father about runaways. He said there was lots of talk, all of it empty, and that none had been seen hereabouts. I felt strangely disappointed at this news.

"They move up a good piece to the east," said Grandfather. "Staying where they're safe from slave catchers."

"But Hattie says that it's a crime to hide one," I spoke up.

"Six months in prison," Father replied. "Not to mention a thousand-dollar fine." He was always a quiet man, but now he looked positively glum as granite. "That's the law, I'm ashamed to say. Some of us obey a higher one."

Grandfather nodded, his white beard bobbing. "'Resolve to perform what you ought. Perform without fail what you resolve.'" His head seemed to hold all of Ben Franklin's writings.

"With fewer Southerners in Ohio," said my brother, Titus, "the law might be different."

The discussion of slavery went on for some time.

The year was 1859 and there was talk that the Southern states might secede. After supper, I carded wool and the others tended to their various chores while Mama read to us all from *Little Dorrit*, the latest Charles Dickens novel she'd purchased from the book agent. Though she strove to impress upon us the beauty of proper grammar and enunciation, she seemed to enjoy adopting the voice of a Cockney or cutthroat or hag, as required. When her voice tired, the volume was passed to Father, then to me for a spell, an honor granted me after I'd shown I could read at a tolerable speed. Proud of myself, I took us to the end of the chapter. Then Mama stood.

"Put away work!" she commanded us. "The New England love of labor has been served. Now comes the hour for idleness." This, we all knew well, meant music. Though Mama could swing an ax and catch a pig with the best of Ohio's farm wives, she'd been raised in the great city of Baltimore, in a fine house, on a brick-paved street, and she was determined that we who'd been born on the prairie should grow up with the sounds of Shakespeare and Schubert in our ears as well as the meadowlark's song.

She took up and tuned her violin. Titus sat down at the piano. He was nineteen. I thought him exceedingly handsome. Lucilla played cello, Ada the viola. They launched into a piece by Beethoven, Mama's baby-filled belly reaching nearly to her music stand. My brother Spencer, three years older than I, turned the pages for her. I sat on the piano bench beside Titus, watching his fingers with fascination. At Mama's request, he'd begun teaching me, that I might take his place when he married one day.

The four of them dashed through page after page, like dogs after a rabbit. When they reached the end, I was sent up to bed. The music rose up from the room below, Mama's violin sweet and strong. Yet how silent her own voice had been at supper, I reflected, during the talk of runaways. I'd noticed this once before, months back. I knew she wasn't one with Hattie's family. She and Father had met, after all, at an abolitionist lecture, during a visit she'd made to Cincinnati. She often led our evening discussions and was forever writing to legislators on education or the poor or women's suffrage. But I knew as well that she'd had a slave-owning uncle in Georgia, a towering tyrant who'd been murdered by one of his Negroes one night—strangled in his own bed. Mama had been a girl then. For months afterward, she'd told me, she'd been unable to sleep except with a lamp burning all night in her room.

The music-making below made me feel luxuriously safe, by contrast. A breeze flowed through the window, bearing the heavy scent of cut hay and cooling my feet. I soon slipped into sleep.

A few days later Mrs. Radtke rode up the path on her ancient mare, Frieda. The weather was anvil-melting hot, and my skin and mood both felt prickly from it.

"How you've grown, *Kindlein*," she said to me. She spoke of anyone she'd delivered as her "baby" forever after. "Tall as the corn. And your hair like honey." She fingered my long braids as if she were admiring her own handiwork.

We walked inside and she exclaimed over Mama's full profile in German, then in English. They disappeared into the borning room. Lucilla and I returned to hemming towels.

"I found Mama talking to the baby, out in the garden," she said. She smiled at me.

I'd spied such scenes often. "It seems a waste of words," I replied, wickedly I knew.

Lucilla's eyes widened. We sewed in silence.

"I also heard her tell Father," she whispered, "that her hip bones were sore and her ankles plaguing her."

Perhaps, I mused, she told the baby the same,

giving it a good talking-to about all the misery it had brought her.

"You and I must keep her from walking," said Lucilla. "We must fetch things for her whenever we can."

I imagined my ankles huge and heavy. Then I stared at my stomach and felt sick at the thought of it stretched out before me like a glutton's. I vowed then and there I would never have children.

Mama came out and Mrs. Radtke announced that the baby would likely arrive in a month. Then she studied Lucilla. *"Sehr schön,"* she praised her. "I will have no trouble in finding you a husband."

Lucilla went red as sunset. She was fourteen and fancied a boy named Jim Bliss. I wondered if I should tell Mrs. Radtke. For she not only led babies into the light but doctored them through childhood and beyond, and then offered her skills as matchmaker, making certain the species would survive in Ohio.

"I shall begin searching for you, *Kindlein*," she called as she rode off down the path.

That night I kept myself awake until Lucilla joined me in bed.

"You're not really going to marry and have babies, are you?" I whispered. I felt sure she'd scoff at such a notion and gladly join me in my vow. Then

17

I glimpsed her smiling.

"I suppose I shall," she said, as if making a vow of her own.

I spun away from her, betrayed.

It was the next morning that I found the runaway.

I was picking berries in the woods behind the pasture and throwing stones at tree trunks, wishing that I'd been born a boy, when I saw her on the ground. She was sprawled on her side. I was sure she was dead. My skin went icy, my stomach hot as lava. I dropped my pail—and she sprang up.

"Lord!" she cried. "Spare old Cora!"

I swooned. My legs felt emptied of strength. Life had filled her body and fled mine.

"Cora's no harm! Don't go runnin'! *Please*, child!"

I gawked at her. She was short and scrawny. Her bony face was as black as our stove. I'd only seen one Negro before. I stared at the tight curls of graying hair peeking under her red headcloth.

"Are you a . . . runaway?" I stammered. Then I saw her shoeless feet and knew. I'd never set eyes on such a collection of swellings and scars before. They looked like they'd walked around the world and back. Then I thought of my family's hatred of slavery. They would feel it a duty and an honor to help her. My unease gave way to pride.

I got up. "My father and grandfather never miss the *Liberator*," I told her.

I thought she'd be pleased, but her eyes filled with fear. "Who's he?"

"It's a *newspaper*. The abolitionists write it up."

She studied me. "You folks abolitioners?"

"Yes, ma'am!" I viewed her ragged, gray dress and swelled with generosity. "You can come to my house and eat with us and sleep in the garret. For as long as you like. And we can find you some shoes, and a new dress too."

She must have judged that I was sincere. She smiled slowly, her yellow teeth emerging. "Bless you, sweet child."

It was then that I remembered Hattie's words. Just *to know* where a runaway slave was hiding was a crime. I was a criminal. If I brought her home, everyone in my family would be one as well. My mind raced like a riderless horse. I recalled what Father had said. Six months in prison—and a fine of one thousand dollars! Each year for my birthday I received but five cents. I'd only once held a dollar bill, and was certain we hadn't a thousand of them. Cora would have to keep to the woods.

"In Canada, won't be havin' to sleep in the day and tramp all night," she said. "Queen Victoria

19

don't allow no slav'ry up there. Reckon I ain't come to it yet."

"No, ma'am," I said. "This is Ohio." The words echoed in my ears. Ohio was one of the free states. Slavery was against the law here. Then I heard in memory Ben Franklin's words, "Resolve to perform what you ought. Perform without fail what you resolve." Neither he nor Father nor Grandfather would turn a runaway slave away. I was certain of this, and felt suddenly strengthened, as if their own blood ran through my veins. "Canada's a good stretch away." I settled my mind. "But I'll keep you safe."

I wouldn't desert her. But I wouldn't make the rest of my family into lawbreakers, who could be led off to prison on my account. I would not tell a single soul about Cora.

I walked with her to the edge of the woods. She couldn't move fast. She'd stepped on a snake the night before and sported a welt the size of a walnut on one of her feet. She said she could use a few days' resting up. I scouted the pasture and the apple orchard, then hurried her across toward the barn. The chickens scattered, cackling so loudly that I feared the entire family would come running. When I led her up the ladder to the hayloft, I expected her to remind me that I'd said she could sleep in the house, but she didn't.

"You'll have the biggest bed of all," I said. The new hay had just been pitched in the week before. "And you'll be safer here," I added. "In case any slave catchers come by."

She lay down on the hay. "Bless you, child."

I smuggled out a loaf of bread, a hunk of pork, half a dozen apples, a jug of water, and Mama's fan. It was stifling in the loft. I found some shoes Ada rarely wore. I searched through Lucilla's chest and pulled out a green muslin dress Cora's size. Lucilla, I reminded myself, had often expressed her wish to help the slaves.

At noon I took food for Father and my brothers out to the cornfield they were cultivating. When I got back to the house, I found Mama was napping and Lucilla and Ada making cheese. I said I'd be off picking more berries, filled my pail with peas from the garden, and slipped up into the hayloft. Cora was on her side. I thought she was sleeping, then saw her eyes aimed at a swallow nest.

"Been watchin' them birds feedin' their younguns," she said. "Thinkin' on my own precious babies."

Swallow wings sickled the air above us. I set the pail down beside her. "How many children do you have?" I asked.

"How many still livin'? I wish I knew."

It seemed impossible to me that she didn't.

"Had me a fine husban' and four darlin' girls." She opened a pod and gazed down at the peas as if at their four tiny heads on a pillow. "Then got sold. New master paid nine hundred dollars for me, 'count of I was a good breeder. Gave me another man for a husban' even though I don't want no other. Master says to us, 'Replenish the earth.'"

She said she'd been sold twice since then, leaving children behind each time. Then she'd made up her mind that she wouldn't give her masters any more slaves and drank a potion to keep the babies from coming. I wondered why she didn't stop swallowing melon seeds, but supposed she knew better.

"I'm prayin' maybe just one of my younguns might be there in Canada, waitin' for me."

"My mama's about to have a baby," I said.

She grinned. "That so! She's blessed. Surely is. Ain't nothin' in this world I wouldn't give to have my family around me." She sighed. "Woman without her younguns is jus' a barrel hoop, with no staves to be holdin' in a circle. Like old Cora."

She told me about her daughter Malinda, who was just my age when she'd last seen her and had so loved playing with her cornhusk doll. She asked about me and I could tell she was seeing Malinda in her mind. I got so used to talking with her that I forgot how long I'd been doing it. I bolted outside and back to the woods, quickly filled two pails with berries, gave one to Cora, and brought the other to the house.

"Just one pail in all that time?" asked Ada.

I averted my eyes. "The birds have picked most for themselves," I replied.

That night I slept poorly. Father liked to say that a good conscience is a soft pillow. I'd obeyed mine, had taken in Cora, yet I turned all night like meat on a spit. I longed to share my secret with someone, then I recollected Ben Franklin's words: "Three may keep a secret, if two of them are dead." I knew I mustn't endanger the others.

In the morning our horses, Argus and Abel, were hitched to the carriage and we all rode an hour to a barn raising. The old men sat and whittled pegs. The younger ones shaped the beams. Women visited. Children played. I viewed them stringing flowers and racing and wrestling but felt no desire to join in. My secret had set me apart from them.

Hattie was there. She sat down by me and fed her rag doll daisy centers, which she made believe were pumpkin pies, washed down with milk from milkweed stems. I'd all but abandoned my doll of late. We watched the men raise the walls with poles and fit the joints together like clasped hands. The crowd clapped when each wall went up. But when Mr. Reedy, in his black Quaker hat, was perched high on a beam, pounding in a peg, Hattie's father suggested it would be just and proper if he used his pole to push him off. Quakers were well known to harbor runaways. A few men laughed with Mr. Puckett. Everyone else fell dead silent. The month before, two men had fallen from a beam during a raising and died. Father and Titus gripped their poles as if ready to defend the Union with them. Mr. Reedy stared down at Hattie's father. Then he finished driving in his peg and climbed down. Murmuring, the men adjourned to eat.

"My daddy told me," said Hattie, "that back in Tennessee there was a man who helped folks' slaves escape. Till they caught him. Reckon he doesn't do it anymore."

"What happened?" I tried to look disinterested but couldn't.

"They split his stomach open, filled it with rocks, and stitched it up again. Then they dumped him into a lake and let those giant catfish down on the bottom eat up all his flesh."

She grinned at me. I grabbed my braids and felt my face go pale as water. For the rest of the raising, and while we bumped and banged down the road toward home, catfish swam through the murky waters of my mind. Three times I failed to turn Titus' page for him at the piano that evening. Without any prompting, I went up to bed, wishing Mama were right when I heard her explain that the ride had tired me.

In the morning Father, Grandfather, and my brothers rode back in the carriage to finish the barn. Ada went with them. She was sixteen and fancied a young man she expected to be there. When she searched in vain for the shoes I'd taken, I pretended to all I'd no idea where they were. She put on her only other pair and strode past me, reeking of perfume. I saw that she was wearing a bustle, adding a ludicrous bulge to her rear. As they clattered off, I vowed never to have anything to do with such a contraption, or any other feminine foolishness. A short while later, I heard Mama cry out.

I ran into the kitchen and found her clutching the back of a chair. Lucilla rushed in.

"The baby's coming," she said. "Today, my doves. I expect it was the carriage ride."

The men had the horses and were too far to

catch. I raced to Hattie's to see if someone there could carry word to Mrs. Radtke. The sky was dark with clouds, the air cool. Their house was empty—they'd gone to town. I streaked home with the news. Mama had put on her nightdress and lay in the borning room.

"Lucilla, dear," she said, "you'll have to go to Mrs. Radtke's on foot. It's ten miles. Much too far for Georgina."

Lucilla dashed off. Even though she was older, I was hurt that Mama clearly had wished to be left alone with her instead of me. I felt glad to be useful when she asked for some sassafras tea and made it up as quick as I could.

"You mustn't fret, Georgina," she said. "Or worry yourself if you hear me cry out. Now see to your chores. I'll call if I need you."

Boiling with energy, I gathered eggs, filled lamps, and scoured dishes. Then I sat in the kitchen for what seemed whole days, furiously mending, my eyes on my needle but the rest of me fixed on the borning room. There were spells of silence, then moans and creaking. I'd never seen Mama in great pain before. The thought drew tears to the brims of my eyes. I feared for her as if she were a child. The groans grew louder. Twice I shot up, determined to dash in. I knew that she would never call me. Then a frail voice spoke the word "Georgina."

I was beside her in an instant.

"Something's not right," she said. "The baby won't come."

I burst into tears. She squeezed my hand. "Take the stoppers from the bottles. Every one you can find. Mother says it helps the baby come easier."

I ransacked the kitchen, frantically pulling out corks and corncobs and wooden plugs. The last, jammed into a jug of brandy, came out with such a resonant pop that I was sure the baby had been born at that moment. But instead I found Mama in even more pain.

"Open all the drawers and doors," she instructed. *"But not the outside doors*. And shut the windows. Birds." I understood.

In and out of every room I darted, opening wardrobes, cupboards, chests. When this failed to help, she had me unlock locks, then untie every knot I could find.

None of this ridding the house of obstructions succeeded in freeing the baby. A few drops of rain struck the window. Mama was feverish now, her eyes watery, her brown bangs wet with sweat. Twice she'd been sick into the chamber pot. I pictured Mrs. Radtke's slow-footed mare and knew she wouldn't appear for hours. Just then there came a drumroll of thunder. Hattie's words in the cornfield filled my ears. Thunder was the Lord hammering a coffin! Mama was about to die! No remedies remained. Then I thought of Cora.

I flew out to the barn, up to the hayloft—and gaped. Cora was gone. She'd pushed on toward Canada in the night! I climbed down, shrieked her name just the same, and believed myself dreaming when I glimpsed her walking out of the orchard, her hands holding corn leaves.

"I thought you all left, like yesterday," she said.

I didn't explain, but just tugged her toward the house and into the borning room. "Cora's going to help you!" I told Mama.

Mama's heavy eyes glimpsed Cora and sprang wide. Cora took in the scene, saw Mama was in difficulty, and felt her belly. Lightning sizzled and struck. Thunder boomed. And once again I heard Hattie's words. The Lord slew *someone hiding sin in his heart.* He hadn't come for Mama, but for me!

"She's been staying in the hayloft!" I confessed to Mama. "I told her she could! I found her in the woods!" With a swift broom I swept the secrets from my heart, that the Lord might pass over me.

Suddenly, rain beat down on the roof as if it meant to splinter the shingles. "That baby's got twisted about," called out Cora. She pushed up Mama's nightdress and began rubbing her belly. I was astounded by its size and the sight of Mama's nakedness. I turned to go, sure Mama wished me out of the room. Then her hand grabbed mine.

"Don't leave me," she whispered. She drew me close and put her mouth to my ear. "With her."

She looked as frightened as a child. Then I knew. She *was* a child, back in Baltimore, in bed, trying to cast out the thought of her uncle murdered in his sleep by his slave, strangled by a pair of black hands.

"Cora's going to help you!" I assured her. "She knows everything about babies." We both watched Cora's hands at work. They were small and soothing, not a murderer's hands. Patiently, she massaged Mama's stomach, distracting us both with the tale of how she'd come to find herself in our woods: how she'd been told in Kentucky to go to a house with a lamp always burning high up in a window, how all the runaways knew that a man there would row them across the Ohio and folks on the other bank would take them to Canada, how she'd lost her way, never found the house, and crossed the river holding on to a log, floating downstream for miles in the bargain and away from the route that most slaves took.

The rain slackened. The thunderclaps grew less fearsome, then faint. Gently, gradually, Cora's hands turned that baby about inside Mama, until the crown of its head appeared, then its face, and then, with a rush, the rest of it.

"It's a boy baby," said Cora. She seemed happy. Mama smiled. Her eyes were closed. I felt shaky-legged from what I'd just seen, as if I'd given birth myself.

Cora cut the cord, then let me wash him, my eyes as intent as Mama's were glassy. I was petrified of hurting him. He was scaly and as wrinkled as a winter apple. I found it impossible that I'd ever looked the same. Then his eyes, deep as night, peered up into mine. We gazed at each other while I finished washing and all during the time I patted him dry. I found myself flattered by his interest in me. I wondered whether he thought I was his mother. I realized that I was hoping he did, and that he loved me accordingly.

"Bringin' younguns to the world, holdin' 'em in your arms—that's a woman's joy," said Cora. I studied him studying me, and felt I knew what she meant.

An hour later, Mama delivered the afterbirth. It was slick and smelly, but after the birth of the baby I felt confident I could watch anything. Cora entrusted me with burying it, which I did, carefully, in the apple orchard. Shortly after, Lucilla burst into the house, without Mrs. Radtke. She was off attending to another birth a full day's ride away. Then Father and the others returned. All were astonished by the two unexpected presences in the room. First for Lucilla and then before all the family, I told the tale, proud that I hadn't turned Cora away, aglow when I came to Mama's asking me to stay and my beholding the birth. Now that it was past, I felt honored, rather than repulsed, by what I'd seen. Neither Ada nor Lucilla had observed such a scene. I felt as if I'd been initiated.

"Strong as a stump," Father praised Mama. "And smart as a jaybird," he said to me. He didn't seem to be upset that I'd made them all into lawbreakers. He brought in a pen, ink, and our Bible. I'd expected to feel forgotten and spiteful when the new name was added below my own. But instead, I recalled the feel of Mama's hand desperately squeezing mine. She'd needed me. I'd helped save her life. We shared a bond none of the others could boast. And while Father inscribed "Zebulon Elisha Lott" in the Bible, I felt my name was being written in the Book of Woman. I would marry one day, as Mama had. I'd bear children, just as she had done.

Corks were put back, chests and drawers closed.

The rag quilts upon which Mama had lain were boiled in the soap kettle and hung to dry, to be ready for the next baby. Then Cora was bathed, dressed, and filled with as sumptuous a meal as we could assemble. She told us that her snakebite was healed, but Father said she'd do no more walking and that he'd take her that night to Mr. Reedy, the Quaker, making use of the moon for light. He hitched up the carriage and helped Cora up. She was wearing Lucilla's green dress and Ada's shoes, and carrying Mama's fan and my bonnet.

"You'll be in Canada in three blinks," said Grandfather. I feared for them, and mentioned Hattie's father and his slave-hunting friends. But Father had Cora wrap up in a blanket and lie on the rear seat, with her back facing out. He told us that if anyone stopped them, he'd say he was taking Mama to the midwife's.

Cora looked out at me. "Bless you, sweet child," she said. Then they were gone.

I strolled toward the barn. I climbed up to the hayloft and found a cornhusk doll Cora had made. It wore a tiny corn smock, with dried flowers for buttons. I remembered how she'd told me her daughter had loved hers. And how she'd held corn leaves when I'd found her that morning. She must have planned to make two—one for me and one for the baby, I guessed. I put it to my cheek. Its leaves were still green and soft and carried the sweet smell of the corn.

The sun was just setting. I walked to the house. Lucilla and Titus were playing duets from Schubert, Mama's favorite. She was nursing the baby in the borning room. I showed her the cornhusk doll and explained. She admired the skill of those same gentle hands that had ministered as well to her real baby.

"It's been a day of deliverance," she said. "Cora brought Zeb here out of the womb. And we helped deliver her from slavery." She stared out at the sky, then at me. "We must continue with that work, Georgina."

That night, as Mama instructed, I lit a lamp, then hung it in the garret window.

3

Grandfather was a religious man, even though he spoke of churches with the same dread preachers lavished on Hell. He had his own manner of keeping the Sabbath. Over the years people heard about it. Some of them simply laughed. Some didn't. I believe you'd have liked him. How I wish he were here. And wish that I'd known that the Sunday we worshipped together that spring would be the last.

It was a gusty April morning, the year that I was twelve. The air smelled of damp earth and new grass. Father and I hitched Argus and Abel to the carriage and led them up to the house. As on each

Sunday, Father would stay home, studying the Bible according to his own lights. Ada and Lucilla climbed up, followed by Mama with Zeb in her arms. Titus had married and settled in Kansas.

"What labors will you commence with, Joseph?" asked Mama. She spoke the same words each week, though she knew that Father never worked on the Sabbath.

"Planting the corn, I expect, Emmaline." This reply varied with the season. The teasing twinkle in his eye did not.

The wind swept over us, chilling my neck. My braids had grown long and heavy as bell ropes, and that week I'd had Mama cut my hair short. My head felt positively light. Beneath it, my shawl was suddenly tugged. I whirled toward Spencer, but he'd already slipped around me and into the carriage. I presented him with a triumphant smile. He was jealous that Grandfather had picked me to stay. Mama gave the reins a shake and they left, bound for the Methodist church five miles away in Beeton. Although she was a churchgoer, Mama never urged her beliefs on Father or Grandfather, or on us. From the age of sixteen, we chose our own church.

Father watched the carriage disappear, then walked inside the house. Grandfather, staff in hand, walked out and took my hand. Our service began.

We strolled first toward the maple tree, stopping before it as if it had addressed us. I believe it did speak to Grandfather, and he to it, silently, for in his mind that tree grew not in Ohio but in sight of the Merrimack River, beside his boyhood home in New Hampshire. If its blossoms appeared later than usual, he took it to be a sign that spring had been slow in reaching New England that year. An early leaf fall meant a long winter there. It was the one tree Spencer and I never climbed.

For several minutes we stood in its presence. The breeze wagged Grandfather's long white beard and ran its fingers through the tree's new leaves. Their stirrings, I always suspected, were for him the whispers of his mother and father, both long in their graves. From those parents, who'd withdrawn, or more often been driven with shouts, from a string of congregations, he'd received his freethinking spirit. The same spirit that had eventually led him to abandon churches altogether and to take up worship in the woods and fields.

We moved on, hand in hand, toward the orchard. Grandfather's fingers felt as rough as his staff, which he resembled—long and thin and strong. Passing in among the apple trees, we gravitated toward those in bloom. Grandfather savored all that reached his senses. Unhurriedly, we admired the blossoms' shades, their symmetry, their aromas. For years he'd had to lift me to view them, and I was proud to have grown tall enough now to peer into the petals on my own. He'd taught me all the apples' names—Russets, Sheep Noses, White Bellflowers, Sunny Sweets, Emperor Alexanders. Like bees, we circulated among them. Though speaking was frowned upon during these services, the eating of apples, in summer and fall, was not only allowed but encouraged. Grandfather felt a ripe apple was an invitation to know the Creator and his goodness.

We moved on and came to Grandmother's grave, a weekly pausing point. As she'd died before I was born, I knew her only by the small silhouette of her sober head hung near the front door. In Grandfather's recollection, though, she was full-sized and flesh and alive, not paper, and he stood a long time before her that day, the muscles of his face moving in accompaniment to their conversation. He then, as always, inspected the pear tree he'd planted behind her headstone. Its fruits were never picked, but rather left to fall upon her grave. She'd greatly loved the flavor of pears.

We entered the pasture, where the sheep were energetically cropping the new green grass, as if they meant to beat back spring. We passed them, then slowed our steps, then stopped. On our left loomed the wall of the woods, out of which came a robin's loud "Cheer up!" A treeful of blackbirds squawked to our right. Beyond them flowed the creek, its waters high and its voice greatly magnified. Grandfather listened, sniffed, smiled. The world of nature was for him church and congregation and Scripture. We looked at each other and dropped our hands. Solitude was essential in his service. It was time to find our own private pews.

He strode down through the pasture toward the creek. Flowing water, I'd learned, called to him. I set off in the direction of the woods. The trees were still bare but for a pale-green mist of miniature leaves. I entered between two sentrylike birches.

Jays shrieked. Squirrels chattered. A troupe of chickadees flitted beside me, seeming to accept me as one of their own. There were patches of snow here and there on the path. Though winter was past, the memory of it had far from melted away, and it still seemed glorious to be wearing no scarf and to feel my feet on earth instead of snow. A roaring wind swooped down through the trees.

Mama had taught me that a young lady of twelve walks where she is going, never runs, but I suddenly found myself sprinting full speed for no reason, feeling light as a leaf, the ends of my shawl flapping like wings. It was 1863. All the talk was of the war. Two Beeton boys had just died at Vicksburg. It was a time of great sadness, yet somehow I couldn't contain the exultation inside me.

I dashed on, floating on the river of wind. How I pitied Mama and the others closed up in church like biscuits in an oven. When I reached a spring I'd discovered, I stopped. Grandfather gave water the same study that others gave to the Book of Revelation. I made up my mind to do the same. For after we'd both returned to the house, separately and in our own time, silent reflection would give way to discussion. What had I observed? he would ask. What new understandings had those observations brought? What fresh speculations about the universe had been given birth to by those understandings? It was on the basis of these conversations that he chose a fellow worshipper now and then. He always listened to what I had to say, as if I were fully grown. Apparently my answers pleased him, as I was picked more often than the others. My brothers and sisters, by contrast, had been found sleeping in the fields more than once, bringing upon them Grandfather's disappointment as well as Ben Franklin's dictum "There will be sleeping enough in the grave."

Woodpeckers drummed invisibly, near and far, treble and bass. For an hour or so I viewed the spring and the creek it flowed into and some water beetles, then dashed and dawdled back to the house. I was surprised to find Grandfather there. Usually he didn't return for hours. We sat by the hearth and he asked me what I'd seen. I told him about the wind and the beetles and finding my first bloodroot flower of the year, and how I'd been too happy to feel sad about the soldiers who'd died.

"Hundreds dead at Vicksburg," he said. "But a thousand births in those woods every minute. They shall all be reborn . . ." His voice trailed off. His eyes had a dazed look to them. Without any more questions, he rose and slowly trudged upstairs to his room.

At suppertime he clumped back down. As always, before blessing the meal, he surveyed the table, then our faces around it.

"Let us give *thans* for each morsel before us." He stopped, and seemed baffled. "For the glad sight of greens. For the taste of hen flesh. For the heft of our bread. For the scent of invisible pump*bin* pies." He halted again, his eyes as puzzled as ours. "May

41

we take for granted no *thin* upon this table, nor any*thin* beyond it."

Zeb laughed, grinning at Grandfather. Ada hushed him. Mama served food, watching him like the rest of us. The words were familiar, but Grandfather's tongue seemed to struggle to form them.

We ate supper early, as always on Sunday. Then Mama, Zeb, and I rode in the carriage to Mrs. Meecham's house, where the Ladies' Aid Society met. While Mama cut out shirts and drawers for wounded soldiers, I entertained Zeb. He was nearly four, quick as a weasel, and a challenge to keep out of mischief. There were half a dozen other women there, all talking while they sewed. After a time Mama led them in singing "John Brown's Body," then "Three Hundred Thousand More." I noticed that one woman's lips were shut tight. It was said she had the finest voice in Ohio, but had vowed not to sing another note until the slaughter was ended. Following this, Mrs. Meecham read a letter she'd written to General McClellan, consoling him over his dismissal from command and assuring him of Digby County's devotion. Similar notes of encouragement to the wounded were placed in the finished garments. While Zeb played with a bundle of scraps, I wrote three or four myself, trying to picture the men who would find them.

"I'm afraid that the rebel states will never give in," a glum voice spoke up. "Now that Lincoln's freed the slaves."

There was much talk of his Emancipation Proclamation, then of the coming conscription of soldiers. I wondered if the man Ada was engaged to marry might be drafted. Mrs. Weems, beside me, was unusually silent. Then she held up the shirt she'd finished and began weeping. She said she'd just found out that her son had lost an arm to a rebel cannonball, and that the sight of two sleeves had overcome her. Mama put her own arms around her and recited the poem "The Virginia Mother." Then, likewise from memory, she distracted us all with a farcical scene from *The Pickwick Papers*, enlisting me to speak Mr. Jingle's lines, as I'd done with her once before. There were grudging chuckles, then laughter, then all sewing ceased as the others gave themselves up to the merriment, Mrs. Weems included. Just as in our house, Mama filled any room she was in with light. I felt proud to be her daughter, flickering beside her.

Zeb fell asleep on my lap coming home. I'd hoped he would. I relished the feeling. I carried him into the house, worried that voices might wake him. I needn't have fretted. The rest of the family, I found, was standing silent as stones in the borning room. Upon the bed lay Grandfather. Ada said he'd been reading one moment, then had fallen out of his chair the next. His eyes were open, staring blankly. One side of his face seemed to have collapsed, like a building brought down by artillery. His lips were moving, but no words were coming out.

Mama and Father both sat up with him all night, taking turns dozing. I could have come downstairs and relieved them—I scarcely slept five minutes myself.

In school the next morning we debated the topic "Resolved: Fire is more destructive than water." I found it hard both to keep my eyes open and to care which team's arguments triumphed. Miss Dirken seemed disappointed in me. Afterward, during oratory, I tried to redeem myself with my reciting of "Scott and the Veteran."

I ran much of the five miles home, revived by the prospect of seeing Grandfather and the fear that he'd have died in my absence. I found him no better and no worse. The right side of his face was still strangely slack. He could shuffle to the privy, but only with help. Though he heard what we said, and could nod and motion with one of his hands, he couldn't speak. Mama had given him cherry-bark syrup. She'd lifted his beard and placed plasters on his chest and brewed him tea from prickly ash leaves. Dr. Cobbett, I knew, would never be sent for. "He's a fool that makes his doctor his heir" was Ben Franklin's opinion and Grandfather's.

I reread him the most recent letter from Titus, who'd given up editing a newspaper to join the army and was serving in Kansas. Then I read him some stories from the Dayton *Journal*, wishing the news were more uplifting. Vicksburg remained in rebel hands. An attack on Cincinnati was predicted. In Dayton a crowd of men had burned an effigy of President Lincoln and declared they would never submit to conscription. Some said they'd sooner flee to Canada than be forced to fight for the Union. I thought of Cora. Grandfather's hand fluttered like a bird in a net. He yearned to reply. I left off reading and instead sat at the piano and played from a book of Haydn pieces he liked.

That evening there was a knock at the door. I opened it, surprised at the sight of Hattie's mother on the other side. Our families had had little to do with each other since the war had begun. I'd heard that Mr. Puckett had offered shelter to Union-army deserters. I didn't speak often to Hattie at school, but that morning I'd told her of Grandfather. She must have passed the news to her mother. Years before, Grandfather had helped get the Pucketts started on their land. During Grandmother's last illness, Mrs. Puckett had been one of the night watchers.

"Heard Abram's out of health," she said. "You all go on and get your sleep." She was thin and deep-eyed and looked sickly herself. She didn't seem overanxious to visit. Slipping into the borning room, she took a seat in one of the chairs and drew her darning from a basket she'd brought.

Father joined her and read to Grandfather—from *Harper's New Monthly Magazine* rather than the *Liberator*, lest she seem unwelcome. I went to bed, waking when I heard his feet slowly climb the stairs. I fell back asleep, then hours later woke again. I'd heard a voice.

I sat up in bed. Lucilla lay snoring. I wondered if I'd imagined it. I cocked my head, heard nothing, then opened a window but made out only the creek off in the distance, talking to itself. Then I heard it again. It was louder this time, a woman's voice. It was Mrs. Puckett's. I bolted through the dark toward the stairs, sure that Grandfather was dying.

"I've talked myself blue," I heard her say. "And *still* you won't admit your errors."

I froze, baffled. Then, weightlessly, I tiptoed down toward the borning room, willing the floorboards not to creak.

"I ask you if you expect to enjoy eternal life and you nod your head. And yet you've followed Satan's path and spat on the teachings of the Lord!"

Her words, and her tone, astonished me. I peeked in the room and saw that she had her own Bible open on her lap, a dozen different pages picked out and marked with pieces of yarn. She lectured him on the importance of baptism. Then on the worship of the Golden Calf. How I longed to charge in and command her to leave! But for a child to correct an adult—much less to order one about—was unthinkable. I bit my tongue. After a while I deduced that Grandfather had fallen asleep. Mrs. Puckett continued chastising him for a spell, then began snoring herself. I soft-footed back upstairs.

She must have spread the word that an unrepentant pagan was dying in our midst. Two days later a church deacon from Lanesville, a man known to none of us, appeared with a crock of barley gruel. He praised its health-giving properties, yet all the while that he spooned it into Grandfather's mouth he whispered to him of the terrors of Hell he would soon encounter. That night his wife took up where he left off. Two days after that a mother and daughter who'd come all the way from Elkhorn County each presented Grandfather with a Bible, then kneeled beside him and prayed for an hour.

Grandfather withstood this spiritual siege. Through nods and head shakings and his good hand's gestures, he managed to convey the fact that he'd not been parted from his own beliefs. His body, however, weakened by the day. He was soon bed bound, unable to walk. He rarely ate. He slept more and more. In Beeton, Mama had seen a notice advertising the services of a portrait painter lodging there for the week. On Saturday Father brought him to the house, that Grandfather might be painted before he died.

He was a cheery man. His name was James Judd. His face was pink and topped with a tall, perennially leaning beaver hat. Spencer and I helped him arrange his easel and supplies by the bed. I felt lucky to have the chance to watch a professional painter at his work, but too mournful at the cause of his coming to enjoy my good fortune.

"Bound for the beyond, are you now?" He approached Grandfather and studied his features. "Rest easy, sir. I guarantee a good likeness. Much experience with the moribund."

He opened a penknife and sharpened a pencil. "I expect you'll bump shoulders with a few of my subjects. And with me, and the rest of us here, soon enough." He began to sketch upon his canvas. "'Grieve not over the inevitable.' So say the sages of India. And James Judd, the sage of South Wheelock, Vermont."

While he worked with his pencil, then his paints, I read to Grandfather, hour after hour, as if my voice would keep him alive. Then I took Zeb out for a walk in the woods, picked a bouquet of violets, and set them in a tiny vase on the table by Grandfather's bed.

That night Mr. Boole, the minister at the Methodist church, rapped at the door. Father had declared that no more exhorters would be allowed to harry Grandfather, but since Mama attended Mr. Boole's church, he felt obliged to admit him. Mr. Boole was young, but stern-eyed as a general. He asked if he might see Grandfather. Father and I were reading beside him, sharing the lamp's light with Mr. Judd. Mr. Boole entered, leaving scant space to breathe.

He delivered a speech of comfort to us. Father, who'd stayed up the past two nights, could no longer keep his eyes open and retired. Mr. Boole moved his chair close to Grandfather's head. He spoke of the body's mysteries, and of the balm of spiritual certainties. Then he calmly commenced to set forth proofs that the Bible was the only word of the universe's only god. Ada stepped in and frowned at Mr. Boole. She was a grown woman, yet even so I thought her quite bold. Mr. Boole ignored her. His voice was soft. He meant to win Grandfather with the strength of his reasoning, not the power of his lungs. He gave examples of doubters and scorners, from Lot's sons-in-law to the Disciples themselves, and their recognition of their folly. Grandfather could no longer move his head, but his right hand disputed with Mr. Boole, parrying every argument.

Mr. Boole asked for cider to wet his throat, then discoursed for an hour on the First Commandment, spiritual adultery, the snares of paganism, and the terrible fate awaiting its followers. I squirmed in my chair, bursting with the yearning to shout him out of the house. I feared I might do so. The thought frightened me. I knew that I dared not do any such thing—he was minister to most of the family. I reined in my rage. He flipped through his Bible, described to Grandfather the lake of fire, then enumerated those who'd be found there.

"Murderers, whoremongers, liars," he hissed. "Sorcerers. *And unbelievers!*"

"And you, I don't doubt," added Mr. Judd. He'd spoken the words that I could not. He gestured toward Grandfather with his brush. "The man needs his rest."

Mr. Boole glared at him. "He needs what I have to say a deal more." He pressed ahead. My eyes grew heavy. I'd stayed up with Father the previous night. My body was ravenous for sleep, but I wouldn't abandon Grandfather. I'd long since stopped reading. Eyelids shut, I heard Mr. Boole describe the torments waiting those who died in their sins. For the first time I sensed that he, and those who'd preceded him, feared Grandfather, that they cared less for the safety of his soul than for stamping out the spark of his doubt, as if it might destroy their own faith. Frantically, Mr. Boole's fingers scurried through his tiny Bible, hunting passages from Proverbs, Numbers, Matthew, Revelation. . . . I fell asleep sitting in my chair.

I was wakened by a mockingbird in the maple. The sky was just brightening. Mr. Boole was gone. Mr. Judd was not in the room. Mama was, standing over Grandfather. "He's been called up out of the world," she said.

My skin tingled. My breath left me, as if I'd plunged into an icy pond. I rushed over and stared at Grandfather. His lips were bluish, his face eerily still.

"Mr. Boole!" I shouted. "He killed him with his preaching!"

Mr. Judd entered, cleaning his brushes. "In truth, miss, the old man licked him," he said. He righted his hat. "The young one gave him the grand tour of Hell, then offered him Heaven. But your grandpap just kept pointing his finger at that vase of violets on the table."

I peered at the tiny purple flowers, thought back to collecting them in the forest, then heard Grandfather's words in my ear: "A thousand births in those woods every minute."

Mr. Judd studied the portrait on his easel. "His eyes had an almost cheerful look to them. I tried to put it down in paint."

Mama placed her hand on my shoulder. "He was snoring, Georgina, and you along with him, when I came down to sit. I dozed off myself. He must have died in his sleep."

Cautiously, I touched Grandfather's hand. It was cold but not stiff, as I'd feared it would be. I picked it up and pressed it between my palms, as if to restore its warmth. As a child of five, Grandfather had shaken the hand of the aged Benjamin Franklin and received the great freethinker's blessing. I wondered what hands Franklin had shaken, looked down at Grandfather's fingers in mine, and felt I was reaching back through the centuries. And just as Grandfather had never forgotten his New Hampshire past or his parents' mettle, I promised him I'd preserve his memory. The chain of hands would never be broken.

Father built the coffin that morning. I looked in on him in the woodshed and found him speaking softly to the planks. After breakfast Mr. Judd's painting was hung beside Grandmother's silhouette. Grandfather was pictured, in a swallow-blue coat he'd never owned, before a maple. I'd told Mr. Judd about the tree. I was surprised to see that Grandfather's face looked much as it had before it had fallen. Somehow, Mr. Judd had imagined it correctly. The bright eyes, I knew, he'd seen himself.

The painter helped Father and Spencer dig the grave. Mama and Ada dressed Grandfather. Then the men came in and carefully lifted the body into the open coffin resting on two chairs in the kitchen. We gathered in a circle around it. It was a funeral with no sermon and no minister. Grandfather believed everyone could be his own minister, so we stood in silence, thinking our own thoughts. Then we all carried the coffin outside, through the apple orchard, and up to the grave, a few feet from Grandmother's. A chill wind shooed clouds across the sky. Slowly, the coffin was lowered with ropes. Ada and Lucilla began to cry. I gazed down into the hole and found myself thinking of the battle-fields, where the Union dead lay heaped in pits. Their war, it struck me, had entered our house. They, and Grandfather, had fought for freedom: the soldiers for the slaves' liberty, he for the liberty to believe as he chose. He'd triumphed. I prayed they would.

Slowly, the men began shoveling the dirt. I didn't cry a drop until then. I don't know why that started me. I wasn't worried about his body or his soul. If there was a Hell, I knew he wouldn't be there. I realized I'd never heard him speak of Hell. Instead, he'd made the earthly world of birds and blossoms seem as wondrous as Heaven. I was certain that it was that world into which he'd be reborn. The coffin disappeared from sight. Zeb pulled a worm from the mound of dirt. I tried to halt my tears but couldn't. I remembered what Mr. Judd had said about not grieving over the inevitable. I recalled Grandfather himself saying that every leaf has its shadow, and finally meets it when it falls. But none of these words of acceptance altered the way I felt. Grandfather was gone. His life was over. For the rest of mine, I could only miss and remember, but never be with him. I cried and cried.

There was no tombstone. That would wait until a carver passed through the neighborhood. When the grave was filled, I placed at the head the violets that had stood by his bed. Then Father dug another hole and planted an apple seedling from the orchard. It would grow up beside Grandmother's pear tree.

Mama put her arm around me. She dried my eyes, then her own. I'd attended funerals before. I'd looked down into open coffins. None of them, though, had held someone as dear to me as Grandfather was. The tears started down my cheeks again. I thought of how he'd tried to teach me to savor everything I encountered—every sight, every scent, every sound, every taste. Then I recognized I was tasting something new. It was the taste of loss.

Mama took Father's hand in her own. They and the others strolled toward the house. I stayed, and remembered my promise to Grandfather. It was Sunday. I walked toward the creek, to worship.

4

Eighteen sixty-five was a year of comings and goings. President Lincoln left us all in April, just six days after the war ended. In May my aunt Erna joined the household. The next month Ada got married and moved to Dayton with her lawyer husband. By then it was clear that this gap in the family would shortly be filled. Mama was pregnant.

Not all the newcomers walked on two legs. That summer Father brought home a McCormick reaper and cut all our wheat in two days. A few weeks later he presented Mama with a Wheeler and Wilson sewing machine. We were living in an age of wonders, he told us. Do you recollect the Nineteenth Psalm? "Their line is gone out through all the earth, and their words to the end of the world." He believed that to be a prophecy of the telegraph. The wires had been run out to Beeton that year. The railroad, people said, would soon follow. Father seemed to take a personal pride in these advances and inventions. So it was that when Mama's condition became plain, he announced that she would no longer be aided by the unlettered, superstitious Mrs. Radtke, but by a doctor trained in modern medicine.

Dr. Roop fit the bill exactly. He'd just come from Philadelphia, where he'd studied at the medical college. Beeton had grown and was in need of another doctor besides old Dr. Cobbett, who'd simply read a few books and started in bleeding and setting bones.

In September, when Mama was in her ninth month, Dr. Roop came out to examine her. He was tall and square-jawed and wore a black broadcloth suit. He was fresh-faced and surprisingly young. I'd heard it said that he'd be needing a wife, and noticed the speed with which Lucilla fetched him a mug of cider. His "Thank you" had a refined ring to it. He followed Mama into the borning room, and I returned to my weaving.

"A *man* looking after your mother," said Aunt

Erna. She was spinning thread. "The notion!"

"He's not any man—he's a doctor," I said.

"He's a man just the same. And your mother is a woman, who's clearly been coarsened by life on the farm and robbed of her last mote of modesty."

This was not her first comment of this kind. She'd always lived in cultured Cincinnati. I held my tongue, lest I be accused of country-bred disrespect.

"I certainly had no doctors minding me." She was older than Mama, which might explain why she felt entitled to criticize her, despite her being the wife of Father's brother and no blood relation.

"No fancy diploma is needed to bring a baby into the world," she stated. Her wheel halted. I could feel her green eyes fixed on me. "I'm afraid, Georgina, there's been far too much fussing over this infant."

I felt just the opposite. The knowledge that a new baby was coming was as stimulating as the September air, and I'd gladly helped Mama prepare. But I remembered, in the weeks before Zeb had been born, acting as Aunt Erna did now. She herself had had but two children, both boys. Both had marched off to fight in the war, and like thousands of others both had died of measles before ever seeing a battle. When her husband received the news, he fell down dead. It was scant surprise that she felt the way she did. Her family had been extinguished. Ours was still enlarging. I'd spared her the knowledge that the cloth I was weaving would be used for the baby's winter clothes.

Father and Spencer came in from the fields and Dr. Roop was asked to stay for supper. In reply to Aunt Erna's barbed remarks, he said he protected a woman's modesty as vigilantly as he did her health, declared that childbirth was fraught with dangers, respectfully disagreed with those who believed Dame Nature to be the best midwife, and spoke eloquently in favor of chloroform.

"I never had need of such drugs," said Aunt Erna. Tall and thin as a cornstalk, dressed as ever in her mourning black, it was hard to imagine her young and full-bellied.

"And no doubt you suffered great pain," he replied. "As many would say that God meant you to do." He faced Mama, his cheeks flushed with conviction. "I say instead that allowing women to agonize needlessly is a sin. That Eve's curse, so beloved by ministers who'll never feel it, needn't be. That chloroform is a providence, a balm the Lord has revealed to man and held out, in His compassion, to woman."

Queen Victoria, he said, used it herself when

Prince Leopold was born. I prayed that Mama would do the same and whispered to her that I'd be beside her. I felt myself something of an expert on childbirth and hoped Dr. Roop wouldn't exclude me. I was now fourteen, had grown a foot in two years, wore my hair in ringlets, like Lucilla, and no longer believed that babies resulted from swallowing watermelon seeds. I straightened my spine, to impress him with my height.

After supper he joined us in making music. Despite the departure of Titus and Ada, Mama had kept up our family concerts. Though I could now play the piano quite well, Dr. Roop's fingers were swifter and stronger and could make the whole piano tremble. The spirit in his playing ignited the others. Mama's bow sped over her violin. Lucilla played cello, Spencer viola. The house resounded with Beethoven. Turning pages for Dr. Roop, I was at the center of a storm of sound and felt gloriously happy. I remembered Cora's longing to have her family around her, glanced at Aunt Erna, and knew how lucky I was to have mine.

Over the following weeks, corn was cut and shocked, wheat planted, and apples hauled to the cider mill. I gathered herbs in the meadows with Zeb, sliced and hung pumpkins, baked berry pies, stored carrots and cabbage and beets in the cellar—most of the time with a book in one hand. School wouldn't start until Thanksgiving, but I'd discovered Wordsworth and Coleridge and Keats. Mama was able to identify the English poets as easily as she could name the forest flowers, and I hoped to be able to do the same.

One afternoon Mrs. Radtke appeared on the path, perched on her tottering mare. The air was crisp, the maple bright as a bonfire, and Mama's belly stretched to bursting. When Mrs. Radtke saw her in the garden, reading a letter from Ada to the rest of us while we dug potatoes, she slid off Frieda, her eyes disbelieving.

"*Gott im Himmel!*" she cried. "A new baby. Why did you not tell me?"

She walked up to us. Mama looked guilty. "I'd every intention—"

"It's the new doctor."

Mama nodded her head. "Joseph felt—"

"You needn't make any explanations. People want what is new, whatever it happens to be. Don't ask me why." She herself looked very old, her fine hair white as milk.

"Enough," she said. "In truth, I came for Lucilla. *Kindlein*, come to me." She took her hand, turned her in a circle, and viewed her from head to heel. "*Sehr schön,*" she said. "He could complain of nothing, aside from this tiny wart on your neck. And that will soon drop off if you but rub a grain of barley upon it, then give it to a bird to eat."

"*Who* could complain of nothing?" asked Lucilla.

"The young man I've arranged for you to meet. He will call for you next Sunday afternoon. He's strong as a stallion and has a fine character."

Mrs. Radtke's descriptions, I knew, could hide more than they revealed. Lucilla showed no interest, despite the fact that she was twenty and unmarried. I wondered if her heart was set on Dr. Roop. We moved to the porch and all drank cider. Mrs. Radtke marveled over Zeb, then studied Aunt Erna and asked if she was married. Then she cast a long look at me. I realized that my turn would soon come. Her bee-like labors in service of fertilization completed, Mrs. Radtke rode off.

The very next morning Mama felt her first pains. This news sent the household into a frenzy. Zeb ran to the woodlot to fetch Father. Spencer rode off to tell Dr. Roop. I brought the rag quilts to the borning room and quickly brewed some sassafras tea. Mama, unlike the rest of us, was calm, and quietly ate a red apple. Her mother had advised her that a diet of fruit would result in a flexible, soft-bodied baby and a speedy delivery.

Dr. Roop's buggy whizzed up about noon. He

strode inside the house without knocking. Hurrying into the borning room, he put down his bag and pared his nails close with a penknife. His hands appeared nervous. Discreetly, he inquired about Mama's pains. Then he turned away from her and toward us.

"I must now ask you all to leave us," he said, "that Mrs. Lott may be free to devote her entire attention to the birth of her child."

I glared at him. "But I was here when Zeb was born! I shan't be in the way!"

Father looked sharply at me and took my hand. "Did you not hear the doctor?"

Miserably, I followed the others out of the room, cursing Dr. Roop. Father and Spencer returned to cutting wood. Aunt Erna carded wool. Lucilla cooked. I tied yarrow and lavender stems into bundles and hung them from the ceiling to dry. Then I worked on Mama's mending pile, my ears cocked toward the borning room. Mama had begun groaning straight away. The fruit diet, it appeared, had worked. I could make out Dr. Roop's steps and his voice. I kept expecting to hear the sound of the baby's first cry, but never did. I sewed for two hours, then could bear it no longer. I stood up, nonchalantly strolled past Aunt Erna, lingered on the porch, descended the steps, then stealthily crept toward the borning room.

I stopped just before I reached the window. Ever so slowly, I moved my head forward, until I could just see inside with one eye. The sight stopped my breathing. Mama lay underneath a sheet, her head thrown back. Her eyes were closed, her skin pale as ice. Beside her was a mask attached to a canister of chloroform. Dr. Roop hovered above her, his hands fidgeting, his face frantic.

I didn't wait to see more. I flew into the house and flung open the borning room door.

"What's the matter with Mama?" I shouted out. Aunt Erna and Lucilla followed me in, gaping first at me, then at Mama.

Dr. Roop stood beside her, his back to us. "I fear," he sputtered, "that she's just expired."

Lucilla shrieked. My body began shaking. I rushed to Mama, clutched her hands in mine, and willed her eyelids to lift.

"The chloroform!" cried Aunt Erna. "I warned her!"

My eyes locked on Dr. Roop. Rage roared inside me. "We were fools to trust you!" I screamed in his face. I stared at Mama. I shook her by the shoulders. I felt I was in a dream and prayed that someone would shake me awake as well.

"I gave the prescribed amount," he stammered.

He seemed to be talking to himself. "I made absolutely certain of it. Just enough to dull the pain." He looked suddenly young and frightened as a boy.

"And what of the baby?" demanded Aunt Erna.

Dr. Roop gestured toward a small shape, wrapped in a blanket on the floor. "Born dead."

Aunt Erna glanced down, then peered at Mama. "Why has her stomach not gone down?"

Mama was naked beneath the sheet. Aunt Erna reached one hand under it and placed it upon Mama's belly. Then her eyes went wide.

"Idiot!" she exclaimed.

She pushed Dr. Roop aside and climbed onto the bed. "There's a second baby!"

I gawked. I put my hand on Mama's stomach and felt the faintest of heartbeats. Aunt Erna lifted up the sheet. Her head and hands disappeared beneath it. The sight of the blood-soaked quilt Mama lay on turned my stomach. I grasped Lucilla. And while we and the dismayed Dr. Roop looked on, Aunt Erna very slowly drew out, by the feet, a tiny baby. A boy.

"He's alive!" she called out, as if we were miles away. "Just barely." His skin was bluish. "We've got to cut the cord."

Deferring to her, Dr. Roop fumbled for his scissors and thread and handed them to her. She tied two knots, then snipped the cord. The baby began to squall. Aunt Erna wiped him off with a towel, then washed him in a basin of warm water. His skin turned from blue to pink. Dr. Roop joined her and Lucilla, the three of them gazing silently and thankfully at this unsuspected twin. My eyes, however, were aimed upon Mama. Her lips held no color at all. No miracle would return them to red. Though I was nearly a grown woman, I lay down beside her, curled like a baby.

That night Father opened the Bible. No one knew what name Mama had intended to give the baby. He settled on "Ellsworth," her maiden name. He entered this and the baby's birthdate, September 30, 1865. Then he moved up several lines and wrote "Deceased" after Mama's name, followed by the same date. We were all crying, except Father and Aunt Erna. The baby howled. I held Zeb tight. And yet, though the house was full of sound, without Mama it felt empty.

No death portrait was made of her. There was a large funeral at the Methodist church. Dr. Roop wasn't invited to attend. Well-meaning though he was, he'd delivered only two babies, we learned. Mrs. Radtke might have saved her. The thought, I knew, tormented Father. His eyes burned. All through Mr. Boole's sermon he muttered to himself. Aunt Erna's manner, on the other hand, had sweetened. I'd half expected her to smirk to see us join her in mourning clothes. But Ellsworth's birth seemed to have changed her, just as Zeb's had changed me. She'd insisted on taking care of him, and held him all through the service. I was glad she did. I saw Mama's lifeless face each time I looked at him, and felt for him none of the affection that I'd felt for Zeb. Aunt Erna, by contrast, appeared pleased to mother him. She'd all but given him life, it was true. After her loss, she'd needed someone to hold. Standing in the churchyard, watching the men lower the coffin, I felt that same need, and found myself now jealous of her. She had someone new to love and be loved by. But no one could ever take Mama's place. My mourning time, I knew, would never end.

5

Without Mama, the house was like a hearth without a fire. The following fall we took off our mourning clothes and buried them again in our trunks, but my insides still felt black. The cold and snow came early that year. The animals huddled dismally in the barn. We huddled in the house. By January it seemed that the winter had had no beginning and would have no end. You've probably had the same thought at times. A great gloom prevailed, outside the house and in. Then Lucilla announced her marriage.

She'd cast Dr. Roop out of her heart and had filled the vacancy at once with the man Mrs. Radtke had found for her. His name was Jari Koskinen. He'd come from Finland and farmed outside of Lanesville with his four older brothers. To try to dispel our own darkness and the winter's, they decided to be married here in the house on the first of February, the bleakest time of year.

It was a fine idea. The household's pulse quickened. Then Abel, our old spotted mare, took sick and had to be shot by Father. That week a letter from New Hampshire brought word that the last of Grandfather's sisters had died. Then Zeb trudged home through the snow to report that three of his schoolmates had been kept home sick. The following day, two more were out. Then came the news—it was diphtheria. The disease preyed on the young, throwing the town into a panic for its children. The passing bell tolled. The churches were filled, most praying for deliverance, others for the dead. Lucilla hadn't counted on this, but declared the wedding would take place as planned.

The sleighs began arriving about noon. I'd hung the front room's ceiling with red ribbon. Spencer and Zeb had brought in pine boughs. Ada came with her husband and baby and a wedding song she'd composed herself. The house was suddenly full of people, as it hadn't been for some time. At two o'clock Lucilla emerged, white as a candle in

Mama's wedding dress. Jari, tall and towheaded like his brothers, looked uncomfortable in his black suit. The vows were read by Reverend Pye. I feared he'd forget himself and murmur "In the midst of life we are in death." He didn't, though he left as soon as he'd finished, to preach at a child's funeral it was said. I was grateful that we couldn't hear the bell from our house.

Before anyone could dwell on his errand, Lucilla directed the party to the food. To our fare had been added fish pies and cardamom bread and cakes made by Jari's brothers' wives. A jug of potato wine they'd brought was opened, sipped from, praised, and passed on. A violin appeared, and produced "Possum up a Gum Stump." There was dancing to this and a dozen other tunes, despite Aunt Erna's wordless rebuke. Ellsworth, thick-legged and new to walking, tottered gaily behind the dancers. I longed to take part, found Spencer was engaged, and finally grabbed Zeb and plunged in. Later, the violin was passed to Jari, who brought forth from the strings a strange, sad music unlike any I'd ever heard. Its scale must have traveled from Finland, for while the rest of the crowd appeared puzzled by the tune, his brothers' eyes and ears were rapt. I thought of Mama's long-silent violin, then noticed tears in the eldest brother's eyes. He missed his country. I missed Mama. On this day dedicated to Lucilla and good cheer, I knew I mustn't follow his example.

The celebration went on into the night. Ada sang her song, to my piano accompaniment. Then Lucilla and Jari climbed into a sleigh, were showered with rice, and drove off, bells jingling. All of a sudden this day, like Cinderella's evening at the ball, was over. Our old life would face us in the morning, and without Lucilla's sprightly presence. I'd slept every night of my life beside her. It dawned on me that what seemed to be a wedding was in truth another death in the family, a leaving disguised with laughter and dancing. I found it hard to climb the stairs.

When I shuffled back down in the morning, Aunt Erna was rearranging Mama's dishes and had placed her own china plates on display. "Do turn out your toes, Georgina," she greeted me. This was followed by disapproving remarks on curled hair in general and mine in particular, on the moral and physical dangers of dancing, the importance of using the word "limb" in place of "leg," and numerous reminders that I was a young woman of sixteen and must begin acting like one. All morning long she criticized me. Then I knew the reason. Lucilla was gone. Aunt Erna felt she now ruled the house and was entitled to instruct me as if she were Mama. The thought sent me into a rage. She would never take Mama's place and didn't need to. As she'd stated so often, I was sixteen years old. I'd all but raised Zeb by myself, required no help with my hair or my speech, and was perfectly capable of managing the house, as Ada and Lucilla had before me. I stormed to the barn, took up the ax, and furiously hacked away the ice covering the water trough.

At supper I dropped a fork. Aunt Erna, thin as a scarecrow, seemed to swell, feasting on this misdemeanor, and declared me in great need of polishing.

"I believe you're confusing me with the fork," I answered her back.

Father roused. "That will be all, Georgina," he said, then returned to his food.

I savored my retort. Spencer sent me a smile. We ate in silence, as we often did. It was 1867 and the papers were filled with talk of reconstructing the South and temperance and women's suffrage, yet once Mama had died the suppertime discussions on the issues of the day had ceased. I noticed how tired Father looked. All winter long he'd grimly cut trees and sawn logs and split wood for the hearths and stove, as if in penance for engaging Dr. Roop and allowing Mama's own flame to die out. Our woodpile had long overflowed the shed. At the wedding he'd sat as he did now, straight-backed and silent, his face nearly hidden by the black beard he'd allowed to grow. He finished, stood up, looked out at the moon, expressed his desire to walk, and set off.

My friend Rose arrived as he left. She said there was to be a séance at the Tuppers' that night and begged me to go with her. I suspected she knew I'd be feeling low the day after Lucilla's leaving and that she'd come for my sake more than hers. I was glad she had, and grateful for the chance to be out of Aunt Erna's sight. Together we washed the dishes. I gave Zeb his piano lesson and read to him in bed. Then we left. I told her about the fork. She halted.

"Drop a knife," she solemnly intoned, "and a woman will come into your life. A spoon—a fool. And a fork—*a man*. Or so they say." She smiled coquettishly, the moon lighting her long blond locks. Then she seemed to recall her vow never to marry and its cause, St. Paul. "'Wives, submit yourselves unto your own husbands as unto the Lord,'" she declared. "How I pity any woman who married *him*."

I was ready to join her vow after speaking with Ada's lawyer husband at the wedding. "I'm afraid,"

I reported, "that St. Paul appears to have written the laws of the state of Ohio. Women can't vote. A husband can beat his wife and owns all her property. He even owns their *children*, and can give them away if it pleases him!" I couldn't help but think of Cora, and was startled to realize that we faced the same injustices.

We marched in mutual disgust through the snow, then forgot our woes at the sight of the Tuppers'. They'd moved into the house when the Pucketts had left. Mrs. Tupper was keenly interested in spiritualism, like much of the rest of the nation. Neither Rose nor I believed in it, and we both struggled to stifle our laughter as we climbed the steps to the porch. The windows were dark. We knocked, were told to enter, and found the séance in progress. We removed our coats and inched our way through the blackness toward the others. I sat down. Rose seated herself on a chair that turned out to be occupied, gave a shriek, then found a vacant one. For the next half hour Mrs. Tupper posed various questions to the departed and asked them to answer with raps upon the table. She then proposed that the spirits tip the table upon two legs. They obliged, all of us insisting we hadn't helped. Next, she held a pencil to paper and requested a spirit to speak through her, which it did at considerable length, Mrs. Tupper promising to read out its message once the room was lit. More rappings were then heard upon the floor. I felt certain that someone was tapping a heel. Rose began to giggle. I feared I'd join her. Abruptly, Mrs. Tupper declared the séance over. Lamps were lit. We all smiled at each other. Then I stiffened. Across the table sat Father.

He looked chagrined. He left with us, not waiting for the spirit writing to be read. He didn't say a word and didn't need to. He'd come in hopes of contacting Mama.

We reached the house. I bid Rose farewell, entered, and found her prophecy had come true. A young man was standing before the hearth.

"Good evening," he said. His tone was rather sharp. He was a short man, plump and red-haired, and was busily rubbing his hands together as if to produce a spark. "Please do come in! Would you care for warm milk? It appears I'm to be the host, not the guest."

"Guest?" inquired Father.

"That's right. I'm Mr. Bock."

Father eyed him in bafflement.

"Zebulon's teacher!" the man burst out. "He who's to draw him out of the darkness of ignorance into the light of learning! Who's charged with forging his character, his moral judgement, his love of country, not forgetting his penmanship, ciphering, reading, oratory, and grammar! For which the town fathers of Beeton provide me a school well supplied with leaks but lacking slates, expect me to make Platos of their barbarous sons, begrudgingly grant me twelve dollars *a month*, and to save paying me enough to live on, send me begging bed and board from my scholars' resentful families!"

Father and I were left mute by this speech. Then I saw that the fire had been covered with ashes. Spencer and Aunt Erna had already retired for the night when Mr. Bock had arrived. He was new to Beeton and had tramped through the snow to arrive at what seemed an empty house. He was cold, and perhaps hungry as well.

"Would *you* care for a bowl of warm milk?" I asked.

He exhaled deeply and studied the floor. "After a vituperation such as that you should rightly serve me boiling oil instead, poured on my head from the battlements." He raised his round face. "Please forgive me."

The fire was revived and milk heated for all. Father apologized for Zeb's neglecting to inform us of Mr. Bock's arrival. I showed him our large collection of books and tried to convince him that we were friends to learning. For his part, he deplored his unruly temper, related his losing his way to the house, then described his last school and its hulking boys, who'd barricaded themselves within the schoolhouse and Mr. Bock without—until he'd climbed to the chimney, put a board on top, and smoked them out. We all laughed. He then spoke of his earlier sojourns. He was twenty-one and had moved about from school to school, like most masters. From a leather bag, as well-worn as his clothes, he drew a book of sketches he'd made during the course of his travels. I studied them with admiration. The year before, in my final term of school, I'd had some instruction in drawing, and had endeavored to train my hand further on my own. Timidly, I brought forth my own sketchbook. He marveled at its contents, sincerely, it seemed to me, and pronounced me his master. I blushed. We talked on awhile, then Mr. Bock was settled in the loom room and I climbed the stairs. It seemed a different house with him in it.

In the morning Zeb marched off toward school, proud to have Mr. Bock beside him. Father and Spencer set out to cut wood. Then the character of the house changed again. Aunt Erna reported that Ellsworth was feverish.

I rushed across the house to her. She was standing, holding him in her arms. He was a year and a half old and rambunctious as a puppy, but that day he looked listless. His blond bangs were damp. I felt his forehead and then the sides of his throat, as Mama used to do with me. I knew that diphtheria began with a fever. I vowed that Dr. Roop would never be sent for. Mama had always done our doctoring. I would prove to Aunt Erna that I could do it now.

I dashed upstairs, found Mama's copy of *Meade's Domestic Medicine*, read through the pertinent section at a gallop, then flew back down, ready to apply a hot mustard plaster to Ellsworth's chest. Aunt Erna, however, had brought, with her other possessions, her own book of medical advice, and was preparing to bathe him in a tub of cold water.

"Dr. Meade," I protested, "specifically states—"

"Hang Dr. Meade," she interrupted. "Make up a gargle of snakeroot and water. Then begin boiling some barley for gruel."

It was not at all like her to use a word as unladylike as "hang." She was clearly worried about Ellsworth, whom she'd largely raised, as I had Zeb. Impatiently, I did as I was told, sure that Mama's book alone could guide him back to health.

She settled Ellsworth in the borning room. She

plied him with gargles and barley gruel and applied scalding-hot cloths to his throat, ignoring every suggestion of mine derived from Dr. Meade. I refused, however, to abandon him to her entirely and sat by the bed, wiping his brow and giving him water. She read several psalms imploring God's mercy, glaring at me as if I didn't deserve it. I knew that she was still angry that the month before, having reached sixteen years, I'd announced that I'd cease to attend the Methodist church and would, like Father, study matters of religion under my own tutelage. Ellsworth was oblivious of our battle of glances. He stared for long spells at the sunlight on the wall, then at a cobweb overhead. His interest in the most mundane things reminded me of Grandfather, who'd never lost his babylike wonder. The thought spurred me further to make certain that he was cured. Slowly, his fever seemed to subside. It dawned on me that he likely hadn't come down with diphtheria after all. Then he began to pick at his throat. A short time later he commenced to cough. By late afternoon he was straining to breathe, at which hour Mr. Bock came in the door. In his arms lay Zeb, with the same complaints.

For the following three days and nights, I scarcely left the borning room. Ellsworth and Zeb both lay in the bed, wheezing and coughing, struggling for air. I cared for Zeb and brooked no interference from Aunt Erna, who tended to Ellsworth. We administered plasters, hot baths and cold, gargles, leeches, puking agents, and bags of hot ashes wrapped in flannel. I stared at Zeb's brown hair, Mama's color, and tried to summon her patience and cheer, but the rattle in his throat as he labored to breathe kept me in a perpetual panic. I knew that a membrane grew in the windpipes of those with diphtheria. Already there had been a dozen funerals for those who'd finally been unable to draw a breath.

In the evenings Mr. Bock sat up with me. Zeb was eight and entranced by *The Black Avenger of the Spanish Main*, which Mr. Bock read aloud with such feeling that gradually the entire household was assembled about the door. He owned a tiny wooden chess set and quickly taught me the rules of play. Aunt Erna felt checkers to be a better choice and put forward the commonly held opinion that a woman's brain couldn't bear the strain of chess. In reply, he inquired of her if I was a competent knitter, to which she assented. He then declared his own mind baffled by the complexities of that arcane art, deducing from this that I should so master chess as to leave him no hope of victory.

Once the children had fallen asleep and Aunt Erna and the others had retired, we recited poems back and forth or talked while I mended what few clothes he owned. I pointed out to him the cobweb that Ellsworth had studied. He drew it in his book. He said he aspired to have the eyes of a baby, and I told him about Grandfather. He asked why I hadn't continued my schooling and I was ashamed to reveal that there'd been no money to send me to the academy in Melton, adding, however, that Mama had taught us to teach ourselves. He praised her instruction.

On the third day Ellsworth's coughing ceased. He greedily drank Aunt Erna's beef tea and soon recovered his energy. Her cures had succeeded, and she removed him from the borning room with an air of triumph.

That afternoon Rose came to keep me company. She said Mrs. Tupper had been thronged with requests for séances by grieving parents. I vowed I would not be one of them. I spoke of my friendship with Mr. Bock and she poured forth advice on courtship, bustles, removing freckles, and reddening cheeks, advice her vow would prevent her from using.

"'She that paints her face thinks of her tail,'" I quoted Ben Franklin. We both erupted into laughter. I told her that Mr. Bock had called me his master in drawing.

"'I suffer not a woman to teach, not to usurp authority over the man, but to be in silence,'" she thundered. "St. Paul," she added contemptuously.

That evening Zeb grew suddenly worse. His breathing was as loud as the wind outside. His voice wouldn't come. He scratched at his throat until I feared he'd tear it out. We all stood over him, save Mr. Bock, who was leading the singing school that night. After a time Aunt Erna looked at Father.

"You'd best send for Mr. Snell," she said.

I went cold. Mr. Snell took photographs, and was often called to the bedsides of the dying.

"He'll be fine!" I shrieked. "Believe me, he will!" I all but ordered them out of the room, placed a fresh bag of hot ashes on his throat and a further pair of leeches on his arms, determined to make my words come true. I heard the sound of Aunt Erna spinning wool. I thought of the Three Fates of Greek myth, one spinning, one winding, and the third cutting every mortal's thread of life. I would not allow Zeb's to be snipped that night.

Spencer joined me, carving animals for the Noah's ark he was making for Zeb. He was quiet, like Father. This toy was his silent offering, his prayer for Zeb's cure. He'd always been good at working with wood. His knife gave birth to oxen, then dogs, then ducks. He retired. The others soon followed. I longed for sleep as well, and for warmth. Though Father had piled the hearth with wood, the winter air was cold as a scythe blade and I almost envied Zeb his fever. Outside, the wind moaned through the maple. I heard Grandfather's voice saying that every leaf meets its shadow one day. Our family was becoming a leafless tree. The wind had already stripped the maple bare. I felt it was now clamoring for Zeb. I closed and latched the shutters.

Despite all I'd done, his breathing worsened further. His hands began to twitch, his eyes to bulge. His face took on a faintly blue tinge. Terrified, I peered down his throat—and glimpsed the ash-gray membrane. Frantically, I tried to get him to vomit, with no success. He gazed up beseechingly at me. I had no further remedies to offer. I felt frenzied. I began talking to myself. I'd sworn I'd save him, as Aunt Erna had saved Ellsworth, as I hadn't been able to save Mama, and I'd failed. He was dying before me. I thought of Mr. Snell. I dashed for my sketchbook. Though my hands were trembling, I knew that I must draw him now, must preserve for all time the memory of his delicate mouth and gentle eyes. I sat down, faced him, but couldn't seem to move my pencil. I felt suddenly light-headed.

"An egg! Two eggs!"

The words roused me. I'd fainted and nearly fallen out of my chair. The voice belonged to Mr. Bock.

"Eggs and a rolling pin! Straight away!"

I tried to clear my mind. Zeb was still breathing. I got up and fetched the rolling pin. Mr. Bock left the house, carrying a lantern, trudged to the barn, and returned with an egg. He held it in his hand as if it contained the elixir of life.

I asked no questions. Dumbly, I looked on as he cracked it and removed the yolk and white. Then he flattened the shell upon the table and crushed it fine with the rolling pin.

"I saw this done when I taught in Pennsylvania," he said. "May it work in Ohio."

He scraped the shells into a pile. Amazed, I watched him put them in his mouth. He hurried into the borning room, tilted Zeb's head back on the pillow, opened his blue lips as wide as they would go, then blew the shells down his throat with all the force of the wind roaring outside. Zeb coughed for a full minute, trying to rid his throat of the eggshells. They flew from his mouth like shooting stars. Mr. Bock raised his back and gave him water. Then the room turned strangely quiet. The hoarseness in his breathing had diminished. The sharp-edged shells had punctured the membrane.

"Once the film is broken, most children recover soon enough," said Mr. Bock.

I studied Zeb. His skin lost its blue hue. And like Rose's prophecy, Mr. Bock's came true. Zeb recovered.

So began our courtship.

"In the midst of life we are in death." The opposite, I found, is true as well. Though he came in a time of disease and death, Mr. Bock made that freezing February into my own private spring. He stayed on an extra week with us. Our evening talks seemed to melt the snow, raise the grass, call back the birds. Since Mama had died, there had been only winter. At last, as it seemed it never would, new life was growing in.

6

M r. Bock decided to stay on in Beeton. I soon knew him as "Clement," and he abandoned "Miss Lott." In the spring of 1869 we were married. I found him no relation to St. Paul.

That same spring Spencer moved to Cincinnati to join the Metz brothers in building violins. Their quality is famous—I'm sure you've heard the name. I was both sad and scared the day he left. I knew that Father couldn't manage the farm alone and feared he'd sell it. But Clement stepped in and took Spencer's place, working beside Father from March to November and teaching the winter term at school. He'd moved in here once we were married and seemed pleased to give up his roving life. I was pleased to see it. I was not a rover. Titus, Ada, Lucilla, and Spencer had all left in turn. I chose to stay. I was the seed corn, saved for sowing. I was quite happy with this role. I would plant the kitchen garden each spring and border it with flowers, as Mama had. I would raise my children to love the woods and words and music and to oppose injustice. I would bring her back to life by becoming her.

I conceived the winter after we were married. The following summer, in the middle of an August night, my eyes opened wide and I knew that my turn in the borning room had finally arrived. I was nineteen years old and nine months pregnant. The pains were mild, but enough to wake me. I both winced and smiled. I'd been waiting for them.

After they'd passed, I slipped quietly out of bed, careful not to wake Clement. I took off my night-dress. The night was warm and the windows in the room were open. I stood naked before one for several minutes. A breeze, sweet with hay, washed over me. Then I rubbed myself all over with a towel. Grandfather called this "taking an air bath" and was said to have started each day this way. I'd never taken one before and hadn't planned to do so then. I did it without thinking, as if in a trance. I suppose that it was my own séance, summoning his spirit to my side.

I dressed for day and crept downstairs. I'd often, over the previous months, spoken aloud to the unborn baby and now addressed myself with "Be calm." They were hard words to follow, as I'd received a letter from Mama's mother full of advice should the baby not breathe or strangle on the cord or suffer a dozen other calamities. To this had been added autumn's approach. Mama had died in the autumn, giving birth. One part of my mind tormented the rest, declaring that I would do the same.

I retrieved the childbirth quilts from their chest and spread them upon the borning room bed. I brewed myself some sassafras tea, just as I had for Mama before me. Clement awoke, bolted downstairs, and rode for Mrs. Radtke in the moonlight. I'd long since made up my mind to have neither Dr. Roop nor chloroform in the house, but to rely on Mrs. Radtke, as Mama had.

Soon everyone was up, followed by the sun. Had I come into labor a few years before, Aunt Erna would have been scurrying about and shouting orders in every direction. But rheumatism had shackled her to her sitting chair and caused her to give up jousting with me for control of the house. I made up a batch of bread dough and served breakfast. I instructed Zeb and Ellsworth not to fret if they happened to hear me cry out. I fed the chickens and mixed pickle brine. Father planned to cut hay that day, and I resolved to stick to my chores as well. But no sooner had he and the boys set off than my pains came on so sharply that I gave up all thought of jam-making and baking and nearly crawled to the borning room.

I'd heard that labor lasted longer with the first child, but mine seemed to move swiftly. I tried to distract my mind from the pain, stared out the window at the maple tree, and counted the points on each green leaf. I was lying just where Mama had lain. My view out the window had been hers. I found the maple before me a comfort, always changing, yet always the same. I felt I was seeing the same leaves she had.

Mrs. Radtke rode up the path upon Frieda. It seemed miraculous that they both still lived. The midwife's back was bent, her steps slow. She entered the room and leaned over me, her white hair carefully combed and kept up with a constellation of pins.

"Good morning, *Kindlein*," she said. "Your day of joy has come. And mine also."

She beamed toothlessly at me. She considered it

a success to deliver the child of a woman she'd herself delivered. Moreover, two years earlier she'd delivered a misshapen child and been shunned by the area's mothers since. When I'd called upon her six months before, she'd looked as if she were on her own deathbed. The prospect of bringing my child into the world seemed to have sustained her.

"I saw, Georgina, several open windows." She had Clement close them. The house was soon stifling. I'd vowed to ignore such superstitions, but knew that Mrs. Radtke would not. She sent Clement out to join Father, which he did with mingled reluctance and relief. She then examined me, and instead of declaring the baby ready to emerge, sat down in a chair and pulled out her knitting, as if she expected to stay a week.

It felt to me as if it took that long. The pains came and went, then came again. Aunt Erna read me letters from Titus and Ada. I watched the sheep graze in the pasture. Clement came in and read from Susan B. Anthony's weekly *The Revolution*, then recited some Browning most beautifully. The day passed as in a dream. Mrs. Radtke baked bread, then fried fish for supper. The sky went dark. Zeb played the piano, choosing my favorite Schubert pieces. I tried my best not to cry out. Then I turned feverish. Then delirious. I felt certain that the baby wouldn't come. I cast aside my vow and begged Mrs. Radtke to remove the corks from the bottles, as Mama had long before begged me. I recollected her account of my birth, listened for hooting owls, but heard none. I was alone. They weren't watching over me. I shouted this news to Mrs. Radtke, who reminded me that Mama and Grandmother had both cried out and groaned and given birth in that very bed, as I would. At once, as if waiting for their names to be spoken, both were present in the room. I had a strange sensation of shifting identities. Grandmother seemed to lie where I lay, filling my form. Mama did the same. Other spirits swooped in and out of me. I felt slippery, changeable, shapeless as a river. I became an infant, leaving Mama's loins. And suddenly I realized that my own infant was leaving mine.

"Ein Mädchen," called out Mrs. Radtke. "A fine girl."

Her words seemed to reach me from a great distance. Drained of strength, my eyes barely open, I watched her cut the cord, clean the baby, bathe her, then present her to me. She seemed much smaller outside the womb than in. She was red as a ham and had a head of brown hair. Her nose and mouth were Mama's own. I felt that I both had become Mama and was holding her as an infant.

Clement and Father and Aunt Erna were admitted. The baby wailed for a time, then took hold of my thumb and seemed comforted. I thought of Grandfather shaking Ben Franklin's hand so far in the past. I told her that she'd now shaken it too. She studied my fingers. I recalled his own study of commonplace things and the value he gave them. What, I wondered, could be both more common and more precious than a baby? I held her, savoring her every wrinkle as he might have held and savored an apple.

Father brought in the family Bible. Clement asked what name I'd chosen, then wrote out "Emmaline Bellflower Bock, born August 28, 1870." Her first name was Mama's. Her second was an apple's, the seeds of which Grandfather had brought with him from New Hampshire and planted here. We admired the owner of the name a long while, then laid her to sleep in the cedar cradle. Father had built it years before. The blanket she was wrapped in had been woven by Mama. I placed at her side the cornhusk doll Cora had long ago left for me.

That night I heard the hooting of many owls.

7

Over the years, of course, there were many other arrivals and departures in the room. Virgil was born, then Jacob, then Rachel. Aunt Erna passed on. Then Father followed. You can just glimpse the plum tree at the head of his grave. Virgil's own five children were born here. Then, three years back, Clement left us. He took a chill riding home from Lanesville—he was overseeing the building of the high school. But I'm tiring myself. And I expect you're nearly finished. I see that it's snowing.

Yes, ma'am.

I was born in this same month of January. The

day might have looked precisely like this one. What a lot, though, has changed between that day and this. Automobiles, telephones, electric lights. And yet, nothing's changed. Here it is 1918 and a woman still can't vote. Over in Europe, we're fighting the Kaiser. A new set of buglers and battles. More dying. It's Shiloh and Vicksburg all over again. But you're too young to have known that war.

Yes, ma'am.

I've got a grandson scuttling through the trenches and a daughter doctoring the wounded. And a son who teaches music at Princeton by day and writes pacifist pamphlets at night. That's Virgil you hear sawing wood. He alone of the four stayed here, as I did. Do you suppose that I might be granted a look?

Surely, ma'am. No trouble at all.

You paint very well. I'm most impressed. I'd been wondering whether my eyes were deceiving me when I looked in a mirror. But seeing my face through your eyes confirms it. I am indeed an old, gray-haired woman, wrinkled as on the day of my birth, lying in the borning room bed, soon to die.

There's no need for you to look so sad. Grandfather had his vase of violets to remind him of the life to come. I have my grandchildren—five in the house, and four more coming by train tomorrow. To touch their smooth skin is to know the future. I've found it a great comfort to do so. I almost feel that you're one of them. You're a young man yet. You'll celebrate the world with your paints for many long years.

May I ask you to take a step closer?

Yes, ma'am.

Thank you. Now perhaps you would give me your hand.